JAN 0 5 2012

Parents and Caregivers,

Stone Arch Readers are designed to provide enjoyable reading experiences, as well as opportunities to develop vocabulary, literacy skills, and comprehension. Here are a few ways to support your beginning reader:

- Talk with your child about the ideas addressed in the story.

- Discuss each illustration, mentioning the characters, where they are, and what they are doing.

- Read with expression, pointing to each word. You may want to read the whole story through and then revisit parts of the story to ensure that the meanings of words or phrases are understood.

- Talk about why the character did what he or she did and what your child would do in that situation.

- Help your child connect with characters and events in the story.

Remember, reading with your child should be fun, not forced. Each moment spent reading with your child is a priceless investment in his or her literacy life.

Gail Saunders-Smith, Ph.D.

STONE ARCH READERS
are published by Stone Arch Books
a Capstone Imprint
151 Good Counsel Drive, P.O. Box 669
Mankato, Minnesota 56002
www.capstonepub.com

Library of Congress Cataloging-in-Publication Data
Crow, Melinda Melton.
Busy, busy Train / by Melinda Melton Crow ; illustrated by Chad Thompson.
p. cm.
Audience: Ages 4-6.
Summary: "Tractor helps Train out of a messy situation"—Provided by publisher.
ISBN 978-1-4342-3028-7 (library binding)
ISBN 978-1-4342-3383-7 (pbk.)
1. Railroad trains—Juvenile fiction. 2. Tractors—Juvenile fiction. [1. Railroad trains—Fiction.
2. Tractors—Fiction.] I. Thompson, Chad, ill. II. Title.
PZ7.C88536Bu 2011
813.6—dc22

2010050150

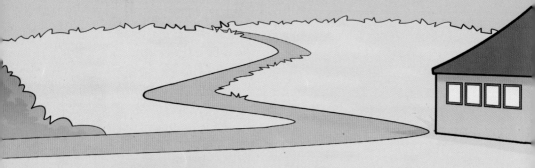

Reading Consultants:
Gail Saunders-Smith, Ph.D.
Melinda Melton Crow, M.Ed.
Laurie K. Holland, Media Specialist

Art Director: Kay Fraser
Designer: Hilary Wacholz
Production Specialist: Michelle Biedscheid

written by **Melinda Melton Crow**

illustrated by **Chad Thompson**

Printed in the United States of America in Melrose Park, Illinois.
032011   006112LKF11

Busy Busy Train

STONE ARCH BOOKS
a capstone imprint

School Bus, Tractor, Fire Truck,
and Train are friends.

Train was not in his garage.

Train was working.

Train took grain to the mill.

Train dumped the grain.

13

Train went back to the garage.

"Help! There is a log on the track," said Train.

Tractor heard Train calling.

Tractor moved the log.

"Thank you, Tractor,"
said Train.

Train took more grain to
the mill.

Train worked all day.

"Way to work!" said Tractor.

"Way to help!" said Train.

STORY WORDS

friends	grain	dumped
garage	mill	track

Total Word Count: 78

11/17/17 Top corner on the cover was glued back. OO.
1/18/22 Tear mended on 2nd sheet + new labels. OO.